Chapter 1

As Katie hurried out of the house one bright sunny morning she was extra specially excited. She couldn't wait to see her four friends and tell them why. She slipped under the wire fence

that separated her back garden from the almost-meadow beyond and hurried through the tangled grasses and bright flowers. Her friends lived in a little house beside the old oak tree. A *very* little house, actually. A dolls' house, to be precise.

You see, Katie's friends were *fairies*!

One night, she'd accidentally left her pink plastic dolls' house out under the tree, and the four little fairies, called Rosehip, Bluebell, Daisy and Snowdrop, had moved in!

As Katie reached the Fairy House, she crouched down and put her little finger on the tiny blue door handle, which Bluebell had sprinkled with fairy dust. She whispered the magic words, "I believe

2

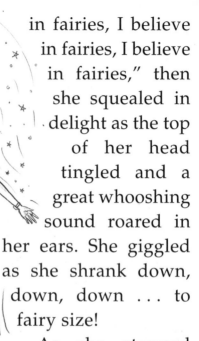

in fairies, I believe in fairies, I believe in fairies," then she squealed in delight as the top of her head tingled and a great whooshing sound roared in her ears. She giggled as she shrank down, down, down ... to fairy size!

As she stepped into the Fairy House she heard her friends' voices, which sounded like tiny bells chiming and tinkling. She followed the sound and found them sitting on the rose-petal rug in the living room, singing one of their favourite songs.

When they saw her, they all leapt

up and gave her a big fairy hug.

"What shall we sing next?" asked Snowdrop.

"Do you know 'Happy Birthday'?" Katie said, giving them a cheeky grin.

"No, what's that?" asked Rosehip.

"It's a song you sing when it's someone's birthday and you can sing it to me tomorrow because it's mine!" Katie squealed, so excited

she felt like she was going to burst.

But the fairies didn't seem very impressed. Instead they just stared at her with blank faces.

"Don't tell me you don't have birthdays!" she cried. "Birthdays are the best day of the year, with a party and a cake and wishes and *everything*!"

The fairies all stared at her, eyes wide in amazement. "You mean you get a whole special day, just for *you*?" gasped Bluebell.

Katie nodded, beaming.

"Wow, you lucky thing!" said Rosehip enviously. "I wish *we* had them!"

Katie looked questioningly at Snowdrop, who explained, "We don't have birthdays, just birth seasons. So, every winter the Fairy Queen gives a big party for all the winter fairies, like me. We have treats like lemon-flavoured icicles and ice skating on the frozen lake and making snowmen and sledging races!"

"That sounds fun!" Katie exclaimed, imagining herself ice skating with her four friends, all giggling and holding each other up.

"So, are *you* having one of these happy-birthday party thingamies, then, Katie?" Bluebell asked.

"Not exactly," Katie replied. "I'm having a treat instead – me and Mum and Auntie Jane are going into

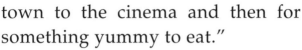

town to the cinema and then for something yummy to eat."

"But, don't you want a party?" asked Daisy.

Katie shrugged. "I don't really mind," she said.

Of course, that wasn't entirely true. Katie secretly did want a party, but as Lily Rose was away staying with her cousins for the summer, who would she invite? She hadn't made any real friends at her new school yet. In her first week, some of the nice girls in her class had talked to her in the playground and asked her to join in their skipping games. But then that horrible Tiffany Towner had been really mean to them for playing with her and eventually they'd stopped asking her to join in.

When she explained this to the fairies, Snowdrop and Daisy looked sad for her, but Bluebell folded her

arms and said, "You could ask *us.* *We're* your friends."

"I wish I could," Katie sighed. "But you know Mum doesn't believe in you. She thinks you're just in my imagination. So I can't exactly invite you to a party, can I?"

Like most grown-ups, Mum didn't believe in fairies and so she couldn't see them.

"But—" began Bluebell.

"There isn't going to be a party so it doesn't matter, Bluebell." snapped Rosehip. Then she turned to Katie and added, "So, how does the happy-birthday song go?"

"I'll teach you," Katie told her.

They all gathered round the little plastic piano that had come with the dolls' house, which they'd bewitched so that it could really be played. Rosehip's tongue stuck out of the

corner of her mouth in concentration as she picked out the tune of "Happy Birthday", while Katie taught the fairies the words. After they'd done a few verses (with each of their names in, because the fairies wanted to pretend they had birthdays too!), Katie was having so much fun that she forgot all about the girls at school. Every time they sang "Happy Birthday", Katie got a bit more excited about the next day, when it really would be her birthday!

When they finally stopped singing (after they'd had three turns each at being the birthday girl), they collapsed into a giggling heap.

Just then, Katie caught a glimpse of her watch. "Oh, look at the time!" she cried, leaping up. "I said I'd go round the village with Mum, delivering leaflets for her exhibition."

Mum was an artist and her bright canvasses filled their little house. She'd recently been offered some space in a gallery in the local town to show her work. She and Katie were very excited about it.

"Oh, please can we come and help?" cried Rosehip.

"Pur-leeeeeease!" begged Bluebell.

Katie was doubtful. "I'll have to go to Tiffany Towner's house," she said, frowning. "If you come along, you must be really, *really* careful. If she

spotted you, you could be in danger. Remember when she stole Daisy and nearly broke her wing?"

The fairies all shuddered. How could they forget? Thank goodness Tiffany had thought Daisy was only a doll, and hadn't realized that she was a real, live fairy.

"I think we should *definitely* come with you," Bluebell announced, "because we might find some way to get one of the other birthstones for the fairy task, or maybe we could even fly into Tiffany's house and try to find out when her dad is planning to knock down the tree."

Even Daisy nodded at this.

At the mention of the fairy task, Snowdrop reached into the secret pocket hidden among the petals of her silky skirt and pulled out a scroll. It had been given to her by the Fairy

Queen just as she had left Fairyland. And this is what it said:

Fairy Task No. 45826

By Royal Command of the Fairy Queen

Terrible news has reached Fairyland. As you know, the Magic Oak is the gateway between Fairyland and the human world. The sparkling whirlwind can only drop fairies off here. Humans plan to knock down our special tree and build a house on the land. If this happens, fairies will no longer be able to come and help people and the environment. You must stop them from doing this terrible thing and make sure that the tree is protected for the future. Only then will you be allowed back into Fairyland.

By order of Her Eternal Majesty
The Fairy Queen

PS You will need one each of the twelve birthstones to work the magic that will save the tree - but hurry, there's not much time!

Tiffany's dad, Max Towner, was the one planning to knock down the tree, so that he could build a brand-new luxury villa in the almost-meadow. If he managed to do this, it would spell disaster for all of Fairyland, and for the plants and animals of earth too.

Katie and the fairies had been busily collecting the birthstones so that they could work the magic to stop him. They had six, but that was still only half the number they needed.

Katie glanced up to find her fairy friends looking hopefully at her.

"OK, you can come." she said and the fairies cheered. "But you really will have to be careful that no one sees you," she warned them.

The fairies promised and double promised, and they even did their

funny little salute that meant fairies'
honour.

Soon Katie had turned big and
was dashing back across the almost-
meadow towards her garden, with
the four fairies flying high in the sky
above her head.

Chapter 2

An hour or so later, Mum and Katie had delivered about half the leaflets. Katie trudged up the drive to Towner Towers with the fairies hovering beside her (Mum had gone ahead to the next house, at the end of the lane). She wondered why it was lined with cars. Was Tiffany having some kind of family gathering?

She reached the gate and stopped still, staring with shock at the sight.

That's when she remembered. At school, when she'd told their teacher her birth date, Mrs Borthwick had said something about Tiffany's being only one day before hers. Katie remembered because she'd turned to smile at Tiffany, but had found her scowling wickedly back at her.

So today it was Tiffany's birthday, and she was having a party.

The fairies were staring too, their mouths wide open.

It was the grandest, most spectacular party Katie had ever seen. She could see most of the children

16

from her class, and lots of others too, some older and some younger than Tiffany. *Everyone* seemed to be there.

Well, everyone except her.

Katie spotted the nice girls whom she'd played skipping with in her first week. She waved to them, but they just looked a bit ashamed of themselves, grabbed hands and hurried off into the house.

"Oooh! This looks like fun! Why didn't *you* come along, Katie?" Bluebell asked blithely. Then "Ow!" she shrieked, as Rosehip kicked her.

Katie felt her chest heave and her eyes fill with tears. Even if they didn't exactly get on, how could Tiffany do this to her? How could she be so cruel as to invite everyone else to the party and leave Katie out?

Then she caught sight of the

birthday girl. Tiffany was wearing a scratchy-looking lace dress, and her scraggly hair was tied up in a ribbon. When she spotted Katie, she began marching over, hands on hips. Katie felt like running away back down the drive, but she stood her ground. She just couldn't let Tiffany see that she was upset. She had to be strong, and pretend she didn't care about not being invited.

"Quick, hide!" she hissed to the fairies, and they dived behind her.

Tiffany reached the gate and glared at Katie. "What are *you* doing here?" she demanded.

Katie struggled to keep her voice steady. "I just came to deliver this." She held the leaflet out to Tiffany.

Tiffany snatched it from her, then wrinkled up her nose as she took a look. "Oh, an art exhibition, how boring!" She screwed up the leaflet and threw it on the ground.

Katie felt really angry then. She clenched her fists and bit her lip to stop herself from shouting at Tiffany.

"Well, as you can see, *everyone's* here and my party is completely *full*, so you can't join in," said Tiffany with a sneer.

"Fine by me," Katie forced herself to reply.

Just then, a shrill voice pierced through the buzz of the party, calling, "Darling angel pops! We're nearly ready to do the cake!"

Tiffany gave Katie a triumphant look and then turned on her heel and marched away. Katie gasped as she shoved a small girl out of the way, snatching her candyfloss as she did so. She began greedily scoffing it, not even noticing that the girl had burst into tears.

Katie looked around at the carousel with its brightly painted ponies, and the huge pink bouncy castle, and the popcorn stall.

The fairies came fluttering up and hovered in the air beside her. Daisy put her arms round Katie's neck and Snowdrop said, "Never mind. It's not as if you want to go to a party of *hers* anyway, is it?"

"No, of course not," Katie managed to mumble. She didn't want to go to Tiffany's party, of course she didn't, but in another

20

way, she sort of *did*. It looked like so much fun.

"I wouldn't go to her smelly party even if you paid me a million gold coins!" Bluebell declared, and the other fairies agreed with her, loudly.

Katie tore her gaze from the clown who was walking round on stilts making balloon animals for everyone, and managed to smile at her friends.

Just then, Tiffany's nanny came out with the cake.

"Wow! Look at that!" Daisy cried. "It looks absolutely. . ."

Rosehip gave her a warning look and boomed, "Absolutely *disgusting*, exactly."

The fairies all made *yuck!* noises with gusto.

"In fact, I bet that cake tastes of rotten fish and old socks," added Daisy for good measure.

Katie gave them another wan smile – it was sweet of them to try and pretend. But she knew and they knew that the cake looked *delicious.* And it probably tasted delicious too.

"Come on, let's go," Katie said to the fairies. "We're not going to find out anything about the fairy task now; it's far too risky for you to fly across the garden with all these children around."

"Actually I think we should still try to go in," said Daisy, surprising them all. "With everyone so distracted, we might be able to get into Max's study again."

"But what about. . ." Katie began, her mind racing with all the things that could go wrong.

But Daisy had ushered the others away. Off they flew, holding hands, shimmering high in the air above the party.

"Hey, wait!" Katie called out, but they were already too far away to hear. Her shoulders slumped. Without her friends, she felt even more miserable. She trudged back down the drive, glum and dejected.

The look on Katie's face told Mum that something was wrong. And when she heard all those voices singing "Happy Birthday" from across the hedge, she understood what it was. She pursed her lips but didn't say anything. Instead she just caught Katie up into a hug, saying, "We'll make sure you have a really special birthday tomorrow, OK, darling?"

Katie nodded, and hugged Mum

fiercely, but she was only just holding back the tears.

Chapter 3

Katie woke up very early on her birthday, just when it was beginning to get light, but she was far too excited to stay in bed. She crept into Mum's room and slipped into bed beside her. Mum woke up, wrapped her in a big hug and said, "Happy birthday, sweet pea."

Then they both sat up and Mum leaned across, opened her bedside drawer and pulled out some parcels wrapped in shiny purple-and-pink

happy-birthday paper. Katie squealed in delight and tore off the wrapping to find hair bobbles, pink socks, a Chocolate Time bar and, best of all, a wonderful new art set full of coloured paper, felt pens, glitter, stick-on gems and stars, and pencil crayons. Katie gave Mum another big hug, and cried, "Thank you, thank you!"

Then there were cards to open – one from Nana, another from Uncle Tony and Auntie Liz, and finally

one from Auntie Jane. As Katie opened it, some slips of paper fell out into her lap. They were vouchers for Hi Ho Silver, a lovely jewellery shop in the town.

"Twenty pounds!" Mum gasped. "That's *very* kind of Auntie Jane!"

"Can we spend them this afternoon?" asked Katie. "You and Auntie Jane can help me choose something."

"That's a nice idea, darling," said Mum. "Right, well, I suppose now that we're up, we might as well have some breakfast!"

Katie got washed and dressed, and when she went downstairs she found Mum in her dressing gown, staring in confusion at something on the kitchen surface. "What's the matter?" she asked.

"You didn't come and make

yourself jam on toast in the night, did you?" said Mum sternly. "You know I'm not keen on you using the toaster without me."

"I didn't, honestly," Katie insisted.

Mum frowned in confusion. "It's just that the jam's been opened and now the jar's half empty, and there are little blobs of it all over the window sill."

Katie stood on her tiptoes to have a look, and sure enough, there was a little trail of jam smudges

that seemed to be heading out of the open window. She shrugged and said, "Nothing to do with me."

"Oh well; I must have been sleep-eating," Mum said.

They both giggled at that. But as Mum put the lid on the jar and opened the cupboard to put it away, she gasped. "It looks like the icing sugar has spilled too. I wonder how that can have happened?"

Katie stood on tiptoe to look into the cupboard. The icing-sugar bag was tipped over and white, powdery sugar covered the shelf. "Maybe it caught on the sleeve of your nightie when you were sleep-eating," she suggested.

Mum smiled, but she raised her eyebrows too. She clearly thought that Katie had been up to something.

Katie ate her cereal as Mum washed up the things from last night's supper. When Katie finished, Mum came and took her bowl. "I'm sorry I haven't made your birthday cake yet," she said as she wiped

down the strawberry-patterned tablecloth. "I've just been so busy getting everything organized for my exhibition. I'll whip you one up when I've put the washing on and. . ."

Katie made herself smile and promised Mum that it didn't matter. "Really, there's no need to make a cake," she said. "I don't mind at all. We can get a slice in town, or a chocolate brownie."

"Are you sure that's OK, darling?" said Mum.

"Of course it is," Katie insisted. Secretly, she did mind a *little* bit, but she knew how busy Mum was organizing the exhibition.

The sun was fully up now and it was turning into a beautiful day. Soon, Katie hurried out to the Fairy House. She was excited about

seeing her friends, especially after they'd zoomed off so quickly the day before.

She swished through the wild grasses and bright flowers of the almost-meadow, but when she arrived at the Fairy House her friends were not outside, and they didn't fly out to greet her. Puzzled, Katie turned small and went inside. "Hello?" she called.

But there was no reply. Only silence.

The living-room door was open and she glanced in. But it was empty. Then she ran up the stairs and poked her head into Bluebell's room, thinking that maybe the fairies were playing camping-out again, using Bluebell's duvet as a tent. Since they'd had the sleepover with her and Lily Rose, they'd had a

big craze on that game. But they weren't there either.

"Hello?" she called again. She checked the other bedrooms and the bathroom, but the fairies were not playing hide-and-seek in Snowdrop's wardrobe or mixing wild strawberry juice in the bath or making pressed-flower pictures for Daisy's walls. "Hello, hello, hello?" she called, but no reply came.

Suddenly she was frozen to the spot by a terrible thought. What if they hadn't come back from Tiffany's yesterday? She'd spent the rest of the afternoon delivering leaflets with Mum, and when they got home it was teatime, then bath time, so she hadn't seen the fairies again. She dashed back down the stairs, her heart pounding with panic. There was only one place left to check.

She threw open the kitchen door and stormed inside, expecting to find just another empty room.

But then four of the cupboard doors flew open and her fairy friends leapt out, shouting, "Surprise!"

Then they broke into a rowdy chorus of "Happy Birthday".

Chapter 4

Katie stared around the room in wonder. There were streamers and balloons hanging from the ceiling and the cupboard doors, and party hats were stacked on a chair. A scrumptious-looking birthday cake sat on the table. So that explained the mystery of the spilled icing sugar and the disappearing jam!

She just couldn't believe that her friends had thrown her a surprise birthday party! When they finished

singing, Katie pulled them all into a hug. "Thank you so much!" she cried.

"It was Daisy's idea," said Snowdrop.

Daisy blushed, but she looked very pleased with herself indeed. "I know you were upset about being left out by Tiffany," she explained, "and I wanted to make you your very own happy-birthday party."

Katie ginned, "But how did you know what to do?" she asked.

"We only pretended to go and search Max Towner's study," Snowdrop giggled. "As soon as you'd gone, Daisy told us her plan. Instead of going inside the house, we hovered high above the party and watched what was going on, so that we could get it exactly right for you."

"Here's your hat," said Daisy.

With that, she passed Katie a shimmering crown decorated with velvety yellow dandelions.

"Thank you, it's gorgeous," said Katie, putting it on and striking a pose.

The fairies put on their hats too – Bluebell had a paper crown with dandelion fluff in the middle, Rosehip had a large red rose petal set at a jaunty angle and Daisy had an Indian headdress woven from wild grass with a bright feather sticking out of it. Snowdrop had decorated

her tiara with paper poppies, and they all giggled when she put it on because it looked as if the huge orange flowers were actually growing out of her head.

Once they were all wearing their hats, it was time for the party to begin.

Rosehip rummaged under the sofa and pulled out a pass-the-parcel. "*I* made this," she told Katie proudly. She went to the piano and the other fairies and Katie sat down on the rose-petal rug. Rosehip turned her back to the circle so that she couldn't see who had the parcel, and began to play.

As the music filled the air, they excitedly passed the parcel from hand to hand. When it stopped at

Daisy, she excitedly unpeeled the wrapping, but there was no prize. "Oh!" she squeaked in disappointment.

"Don't worry, there's not always a prize in every layer; you've got plenty more chances yet!" Katie promised her, and Daisy raised a smile.

But when Katie got the parcel herself, there wasn't a prize in that layer either, and there wasn't when Snowdrop got it, or when Bluebell had a turn or when Daisy got it again (and she really *was* upset then).

By the time Bluebell got the package again, it was getting very small. She tore off the shiny

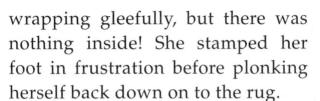

wrapping gleefully, but there was nothing inside! She stamped her foot in frustration before plonking herself back down on to the rug.

"Erm, Rosehip, did you. . ." Katie began, but Rosehip had started to play again, and didn't hear her. *Of course*, Katie thought to herself, *she must have just put one big prize in the middle.* Her tummy flipped over with excitement. They were just about on the last layer now. Then the music stopped and *she* got the parcel! She tore into the wrapping, desperate to find out what her prize would be.

But, apart from a screwed-up ball of wrapping paper, there was nothing.

"You know, I thought this game would be more fun," said Snowdrop, frowning at the ripped

pile of coloured wrapping.

"Erm, it would have been, if Rosehip had put any prizes in the parcel!" Katie exclaimed.

"You silly thing, Rosehip!" said Bluebell crossly.

"I didn't know about putting prizes in!" Rosehip harrumphed, tossing her flame-red hair crossly. "I only watched this game for a minute and I didn't see the end. Anyway, it was called *pass the parcel*, not *pass the parcel and win prizes*, so how was *I* supposed to know? It's not *my* fault!"

"It doesn't matter," Katie forced herself to say, even though she was very disappointed about not getting a prize. "It was a lovely idea. You

just didn't quite understand it, that's all."

But Bluebell and Rosehip were still glaring at each other.

"Let's play something else," Katie suggested then. "How about Chinese whispers?"

"How do you play that?" Daisy asked.

"One of us whispers something to the person next to her, and then we pass it round the circle and see if it comes out the same at the end," Katie explained. "It's one of my favourite games!"

"That sounds like fun," said Snowdrop, and even Bluebell and Rosehip looked keen. So they sat back down on the rose-petal rug and Rosehip volunteered to begin. She whispered to Daisy and Daisy whispered to Katie and Katie

whispered to Snowdrop and Snowdrop whispered to Bluebell. And Bluebell leapt to her feet and shrieked, "'*Bluebell the fairy smells?!*' That's a horrible thing to whisper, Rosehip!"

Rosehip also leapt up, her flame-red hair flying. "I whispered, 'Use bluebells for fairy spells', *actually*!" she screeched. "Someone probably misheard it – that's how the game *work*s, Bluebell!"

"I don't believe you. I bet you did say I smell in the first place," Bluebell accused, stamping her foot crossly.

"Didn't!" cried Rosehip.

"Did!" yelled Bluebell.

"Didn't!"

"Did!"

"Didn't!"

"Did!"

One of their famous fights was

42

threatening to break out, and Katie noticed that poor Snowdrop and Daisy were looking rather upset about it. "It was nice of you to make me a cake," Katie said to Daisy, to distract her.

"Let's have some, shall we?" The summer fairy suggested, cheering up a bit.

At the mention of cake, the other two fairies soon forgot their quarrel, and when Daisy led the way into the kitchen, they skipped along behind her.

Chapter 5

The cake that Daisy had baked looked absolutely beautiful. It was covered in white icing and oozing with borrowed jam, and there were eight candles on top of it. They all gathered round as Snowdrop sprinkled a smidgen of fairy dust on to the candles. Katie gasped as a magical flame sprung from each one.

She closed her eyes to make her birthday wish . . . but then opened them again suddenly. The candles were making a strange spluttering sound. She peered at them, saying, "Hang on, these candles don't sound quite right."

"*Candles?*" repeated Daisy in puzzlement. "What are *candles*? These are fairy fireworks, just like on the birthday cake that we saw at Tiffany's party. Come on, make your wish!"

Katie winced. "Quick, get down – it's going to—"

BOOM!!!!

In a shower of silver sparkles, the cake blew up.

The fairies screamed and

shot into the air. Cake went flying all over the kitchen. It covered the cupboards, smudged the pretty pressed-flower pictures and splattered all over the pink chequered tablecloth. Globs of sticky icing slid down the windows and clung to the polka-dot curtains.

Snowdrop just stared at the mess with her mouth hanging open, totally in shock.

Rosehip stifled a giggle.

Bluebell licked some icing off her arm and said, "Yum! It's still tasty!"

But poor Daisy was devastated. "I didn't know

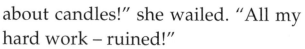

about candles!" she wailed. "All my hard work – ruined!"

"It doesn't matter," Katie said quietly, trying to hide her disappointment. She really had wanted to make a birthday wish and taste the delicious-looking cake.

Snowdrop put her arm round Daisy. "Let's leave the clearing up for now," she said softly. "Shall we go into the living room and have another game?"

"Good idea! How about musical chairs!" suggested Rosehip brightly.

Even Daisy managed a small smile at this suggestion, and they all hurried back into the living room.

Katie explained the rules of musical chairs, just to make double-sure that they all understood the game this time. Then she set out the four plastic chairs that had come

with the dolls' house, which the fairies had painted purple and covered in silver sparkles. Rosehip really wanted to join in too, so Snowdrop took the little bottle of fairy dust from the secret pocket in her silky petal skirt and sprinkled some on to the piano keys.

Katie gasped in amazement as the bewitched instrument began chiming out one of their favourite fairy songs, all on its own. The four fairies and Katie started skipping and dancing around the chairs. When the music stopped, they all dived for a chair, and Snowdrop was out first. She was soon followed by Daisy in the next round. Then Katie herself was caught without a chair, and she hurried to the wall to join the others. None of them minded being out, because they'd had so much fun playing the game.

They all cheered Bluebell and Rosehip on as they danced and pranced around the last chair. But as the music stopped both fairies planted themselves firmly down on it at exactly the same time and absolutely refused to budge.

"I got here first!" cried Bluebell, poking Rosehip in the ribs.

"No, *I* did!" Rosehip insisted, giving Bluebell a swift kick.

"No, it was me!" shouted Bluebell.

"Anyway, it's not who was first, it's how long you can stay on the chair," said Rosehip then.

Katie sighed and rolled her eyes – it was typical of these two to start making up their own rules.

"Fine. Then I'll stay here all afternoon!" said Bluebell, folding her arms.

"Well, *I'll* stay here all week!" Rosehip insisted.

"Well, I'll stay here all *year*!" said Bluebell, giving Rosehip a smug look.

"A year is a *very* long time to sit on a chair," Daisy pointed out. So Bluebell had another think and then she said, "Anyway, it's not that; it's the person who's got more of herself *on* the chair who wins." And with that she shoved Rosehip off.

"Eeeeekkk!!!!" Rosehip squealed.

"Hey!" cried Daisy.

Rosehip picked herself up from the floor, looking really cross, and pinched Bluebell on the arm until she fell off the chair sideways.

"Stop it, you two!" Daisy wailed, but they didn't seem to hear. Instead they both set about trying to push each other off the chair, wings flapping and arms flailing.

"Don't! You're spoiling Katie's happy-birthday party!" cried Daisy, but they still didn't take any notice. That was, until she burst into tears.

The two naughty fairies finally stopped pushing and shoving. Katie and Snowdrop put their arms round

Daisy, who was sobbing hard now. Rosehip and Bluebell hung their heads and looked very ashamed of themselves indeed. "We're sorry, Daisy," whispered Bluebell.

"We really are," mumbled Rosehip.

Katie tried to cheer things up. "I know, let's open my presents," she said brightly. "That will be fun."

But the fairies just looked puzzled.

"What presents?" asked Bluebell.

"You must mean packages like the ones we saw at Tiffany's!" cried Snowdrop. "Oh! Erm. . ." She trailed off, looking at the floor.

Katie turned to Rosehip, who muttered, "Well, it's just we didn't know they were presents, we thought they were spare pass-the-parcels."

"So, no presents then?" said Katie glumly.

Bluebell shuffled awkwardly. "Erm, no . . . sorry," she said finally.

"Oh, what a disaster!" Daisy wailed. "I wanted to make you a perfect happy-birthday party but everything has gone wrong!"

The four fairies plonked themselves down on the musical chairs, looking glummer than Katie had ever seen them. She knew that she ought to think of something to cheer them all up and save the day. But she just couldn't, because she felt completely

miserable herself. It had been the worst birthday party *ever*: her cake had exploded, there were no prizes in her pass-the-parcel, Rosehip and Bluebell had fought over the other games, and now there weren't any presents.

She sighed as she watched the last dandelion drop from her crown on to the floor at her feet. Even her party hat was falling to pieces.

"Erm, I think I'd better head home," she said quietly. "Mum's expecting me back, to go into town."

When she slipped out of the room, the fairies were so down in the dumps that they didn't even say goodbye.

Chapter 6

When Katie got back from her visit to town with Mum and Auntie Jane she felt much better, and she couldn't wait to tell the fairies all about it. She hoped they weren't still upset about her birthday party going so terribly wrong – after all, they really had done their best, and it was the thought that counted.

She wanted to tell them all about the funny film she'd seen in the cinema, and the pizza she'd shared

with Auntie Jane, and how the waiter had brought out a chocolate brownie with a candle in it and the whole restaurant had joined in with singing "Happy Birthday" to her.

She also wanted to show them her beautiful new fairy wings. She'd spotted them in the window of a toy shop and she'd just *had* to go in and try them on. When Mum had seen how nice they looked, she'd bought them for her as an extra little present. Of course they couldn't fly like real fairy wings, but they'd be fun for let's-pretend games and, while wearing them, Katie could almost imagine she was a fairy herself.

But Katie had a far more important reason for visiting the fairies. She had something to give them. Something that was a

surprise. Something that was very special indeed.

And she didn't know it, but back at the Fairy House, her four friends had been hatching a plan to do something very special for *her* too.

As Katie neared the Fairy House, she could see lots of flags, flapping in the breeze beside it. They were made of straws and scraps of material. Two of the kitchen chairs had been pulled outside and decorated with gold and silver glitter. The front door was thrown open and cheery piano music drifted out of it. Strange exotic flowers were growing out of the ground, and Katie could tell at once that they had been put there by magic. Her stomach flipped with excitement. What on earth were her friends up to?

When she reached the Fairy House, she carefully stepped over

the flags and flowers, then touched the enchanted door handle and whispered the magic words that would shrink her down to fairy size. Just as she was going into the house, the fairies all came bursting out of it, beaming.

"Welcome to your magical fairy party!" cried Bluebell, giving her a big hug.

"We were so bad at making you a happy-birthday party, we thought we'd stick to what we know and throw you a fairy party instead," Snowdrop explained. "I hope that's OK," she added shyly.

Katie's eyes shone with excitement. "Of course it's OK! It's brilliant!" she cried. "I'd far rather have a fairy party! I must be the only girl in the world to have *ever* had one!"

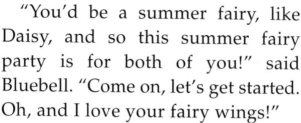

"You'd be a summer fairy, like Daisy, and so this summer fairy party is for both of you!" said Bluebell. "Come on, let's get started. Oh, and I love your fairy wings!"

Soon they were sitting next to each other on the glittery chairs, wearing several daisy chains each.

As the others danced around them, Katie felt like a princess in some far away magical land. She and Daisy

beamed at each other. The disaster of the morning had been left far behind, and the smile on Daisy's freckled face was the biggest, widest grin she'd ever seen.

As the other three fairies skipped and danced round the chairs, they began to sing a special song for Katie and Daisy, which went like this:

"Sunshine and daisies and buttercups yellow
Long lazy days playing in the green meadow
Magpies and butterflies fluttering by
Sweet summer fairies fly high in the sky.

The kind summer fairy loves laughter and hugs
She cares about others and cheers people up

So thanks, summer fairies, for spending your time
Bringing sunshine and laughter and fun to our lives!"

Katie beamed, feeling absolutely and utterly like the luckiest girl in the world. Here she was with her four best friends, at a magical enchanted fairy party they had thrown especially for her and Daisy. She was so happy she thought she might burst.

After the summer fairy song, they all played skipping games and they had relay races where you hopped to a bucket and then put it on your head and skipped back. They all started giggling when

Bluebell bumped into a flagpole and fell over, and they just couldn't stop! Soon they were so doubled up with laughter that none of them could even stand upright, let alone hop!

When they had calmed down a little bit, Daisy went in and fetched a big plate piled high with fairy cakes, and Snowdrop brought out a huge jug of wild strawberry sparkle-shake surprise, which she'd made herself. She poured the magic drink out into acorn cups and Katie took a big sip, then giggled as a swoosh of sparkly bubbles came streaming out of her mouth, just as they had at the Fairy Sleepover.

Daisy's fairy cakes looked beautiful, with shiny icing in jewel-bright colours and a sparkly sweet gem in the centre of each. And they had a magical surprise in them, too!

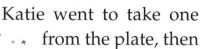

Katie went to take one from the plate, then she gasped in surprise as it lifted into the air and began floating away. "Fairy cakes are so light you have to be quick to catch them!" giggled Daisy, then she zoomed off after a little cake with yellow icing and a pink gem on top.

Rosehip offered to catch Katie a cake, but Snowdrop had a better idea. She pulled the bottle of fairy dust from among the folds of her silky petal skirt. "It won't last too long, but here," she said, shaking some fairy dust out on to Katie's new wings. Suddenly they came to life, flapping all on their own. Katie found that she just had to think about flying

and the wings took her into the air.

"Wow!" she squealed in delight, "this is just like being a real fairy!"

She twirled and spun in the sky, then zoomed after a cake with emerald-green icing and a purple diamond-shaped gem. She popped it into her mouth and it tasted like, well, like nothing she'd ever tasted before – a mixture of vanilla and chocolate and strawberry and *magic*.

Katie and the fairies twirled and tumbled and shrieked and giggled, chasing after the cakes, until the only ones they hadn't caught were too far away in the distance to go after. They fell to the

ground in a puffed-out heap, laughing and clutching their tummies. "Oh-er!" said Daisy, as she began to float back into the air. "I think I ate a few too many!"

That set them all off giggling again,

and Daisy had to cling to one of the flagpoles to stop herself from floating away.

"Let's play something indoors until Daisy comes down to earth," suggested Snowdrop, and they all agreed that that was a very good idea. After all, they didn't want their best friend disappearing on the breeze, did they?

They decided to play hide-and-seek and Katie volunteered to be the finder. She counted to one hundred before going up the stairs, but it didn't take long to find the fairies. The wardrobe in Snowdrop's room was swaying and

banging, and a fairy foot was poking out.

"Shhh!" Bluebell hissed loudly, "or she'll hear us!!!"

Katie smiled to herself, tiptoed up and threw open the wardrobe door. "Found you!" she cried. Snowdrop, Bluebell and Rosehip spilled out, and Daisy went bobbing up to the ceiling.

"How on earth did you find us so quickly when we were being so quiet?" asked Bluebell in amazement.

Katie shrugged, hiding a grin. "Oh, just luck, I suppose," she said.

Then Snowdrop was the finder and Katie hid with the others under Bluebell's bed. She had to keep a tight hold on Daisy to stop her floating out and giving them away. It took Snowdrop ages to find them this time.

They played once more, and when Bluebell finally found the others all squashed behind the bathroom door, Daisy had stopped floating and was almost completely back to normal.

They went outside again, blinking in the blazing afternoon sunshine, and played tag in the air, tumbling and zooming and shrieking, until the fairy dust magic wore off Katie's wings.

As they were getting their breath back, she remembered something. She'd forgotten it in all the excitement. It was the very important surprise she'd brought for the fairies. The reason she'd come down to the Fairy House in the first place. "I've got a surprise for you," she told her friends. She went over to the front door and picked up a carrier bag,

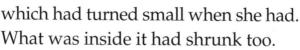

which had turned small when she had. What was inside it had shrunk too.

She took the surprise out of the bag and the fairies stared at it. It was a pass-the-parcel. "Seeing as this game went so wrong this morning, I thought we could have another try," she said.

They all squealed and rushed back inside to sit on the rose-petal rug, and Snowdrop sprinkled some more fairy dust on the piano to make it magically play for them again. Soon the parcel was passing from hand to hand. There were a few sweets in some of the layers, and nothing in others, but no one minded too much what they got. It was the fun of playing the game that counted.

When they got down to the last layer, they were so excited they

could barely sit still.

They passed the parcel round and round and round, and Bluebell lingered over it so much on her turn that Rosehip told her to hurry up, and then when the music finally stopped it was *Daisy* holding the package, and she looked so surprised to see it in her hands that it made them all giggle.

She opened the wrapping carefully and they all leaned in to see what the

prize was. As she unpicked the last piece of tape, the paper fell open and something silvery slithered into her lap. She lifted it up and everyone gasped at the bluey-green gemstone necklace, glinting in the sunlight from the window.

"Wow! That's beautiful," cried Bluebell.

"Gorgeous!" Snowdrop agreed.

Katie grinned. "Look closer," she told them. They all peered at the necklace, puzzled. Daisy was the first to understand. "It's . . . Katie, it's not, is it? Oh, Katie! Thanks!" she squealed.

"You're welcome," Katie said, but the other fairies were still peering at the necklace, confused,

until Bluebell suddenly shouted, "It's aquamarine! You got us one of the birthstones that we need to work the magic to save the tree!"

They all squealed, and Katie explained about the vouchers from Auntie Jane. "I couldn't believe my luck when I spotted the aquamarine necklace in Hi Ho Silver," she told them. "I just had to buy it!"

She couldn't help grinning. The present she'd *given* had made her happier than all the ones she'd received put together. Now they had seven birthstones, and they were one step closer to saving the Magic Oak and Fairyland itself.

Katie glowed with happiness, "This has been my best birthday ever!" she cried. And they all had a big fairy hug.

The End

COME AND JOIN
YOUR FAIRY FRIENDS!

For fantastic competitions,
exclusive material and lots more fairy fun,
enter the Fairy House now!

www.thefairyhouse.co.uk

For

Fabienne and Angelica,
with love

FIFE COUNCIL		
841772		
Fii	PETERS	26-Jun-2008	s
	JF	£5.99
Reg SCHOLAS'	JF	BAND	A demarks

Text copyright © Kelly McKain, 2008
Illustration copyright © Nicola Slater, 2008

The right of Kelly McKain and Nicola Slater to be identified as the author and illustrator of this work have been asserted by them.

Cover illustration © Nicola Slater, 2008

ISBN 978 1 407 10640 3

A CIP catalogue record for this book
is available from the British Library
All rights reserved
This book is sold subject to the condition that it shall
not, by way of trade or otherwise, be lent, hired out or otherwise circulated in
any form of binding or cover other than that in which it is published. No part
of this publication may be reproduced, stored in a retrieval system, or
transmitted in any form or by any means (electronic, mechanical,
photocopying, recording or otherwise) without
the prior written permission of
Scholastic Limited.

Printed and bound by Imago
Papers used by Scholastic Children's Books are made from
wood grown in sustainable forests.

1 3 5 7 9 10 8 6 4 2

This is a work of fiction. Names, characters, places, incidents and dialogues are
products of the author's imagination or are used fictitiously. Any resemblance to
actual people, living or dead, events or locales is entirely coincidental.

www.kellymckain.co.uk
www.scholastic.co.uk/zone

The Fairy House
Fairy Party

Kelly McKain

Illustrated by Nicola Slater

MSCHOLASTIC

Look out for all *The Fairy House* books:

FAIRY FRIENDS
FAIRY FOR A DAY
FAIRIES TO THE RESCUE
FAIRY RIDING SCHOOL
FAIRY SLEEPOVER
FAIRY JEWELS
FAIRY PARTY
FAIRY FLYING LESSONS

Other books by Kelly McKain

Mermaid Rock:
PIRATE TROUBLE
SPOOKY SHIPWRECK
TREASURE HUNT
WHALE RESCUE

Make sure you visit www.thefairyhouse.co.uk
for competitions, prizes and lots more fairy fun!
www.kellymckain.co.uk

KU-147-929

The Fairy House
Fairy Party

Welcome to the Fairy House –
a whole new magical world...